THE CANDIDATE'S MAID
Part Two

The Colonel's
Secret Service

THE CANDIDATE'S MAID
Part Two

The Colonel's Secret Service

LAURA LIS SCOTT

Toot Sweet Ink
tootsweet.ink

Boulder

A Toot Sweet Ink Book
Published by Toot Sweet Inc.
6525 Gunpark Drive Suite 370
Boulder, CO 80301

Visit us at tootsweet.ink

Toot Sweet Ink is a trademark of Toot Sweet Inc.

Library of Congress Control Number: 2016908120
First Edition

ISBN: 978-1-943194-12-4 (hardback)
ISBN: 978-1-943194-11-7 (trade paper)

To Mom,
who has always believed

THE CANDIDATE'S MAID
Part Two

Contents

THE CANDIDATE'S MAID
Part Two

The Colonel's
Secret Service

1

I CAN TELL YOU THIS: I didn't actually scream. I was too busy trying to breathe as we barreled down the mountain in Mr. Henderson's custom snow jalopy—a supercar on treads and skis. Heavy snow splatted against the windshield, and the wipers flailed back and forth, flinging it off to the sides. With the sunlight's glare, I couldn't see anything beyond a few feet past the hood. So when the garbage-truck-sized boulder appeared, I had time only to gasp and blink.

Mr. Henderson swerved. The granite shot past my window. He bellowed with excitement as we hurtled through a stand of scraggly trees into a giant swale leading to a steep rise covered with hundred-foot maples.

I tried to get into the spirit. You know how there is nothing more beautiful than fresh, argent snow? How brilliantly it dazzles in sunshine under an azure sky? Fields are downy pillows. Trees are flocked like cotton sentinels.

It's not so idyllic, I can assure you, when you're bouncing across snow drifts and slaloming between tree trunks at seventy miles an hour.

The engine—a high-revving, turbocharged BMW V6, Mr. Henderson boasted—blared and moaned as the snow beast sped up a steep hill. "Come on, Gretchen," he coaxed. (That's what he called this thing: Gretchen—in honor Gretchen Fraser, the first American skier to win Olympic gold. How could anyone feel unsafe in something so sentimentally patriotic?)

I mentally forced my white-knuckled hand to let go of the roll cage and reach into my bag. The bundle of money was still there. I ran my finger along the top edge of the stack of hundreds. I don't know if you've ever fondled ten thousand dollars in cash, but I can tell you, it feels really nice—like a clump of security.

I peeked at my phone. 2:13 PM. The train was coming any moment. When, we weren't sure. Soon. And it would possibly be the last train for who knew how long. A second nor'easter was poised to sweep in. This was my last chance for days to get back to New York City and prevent being evicted from my apartment.

"Don't you worry," Mr. Henderson said. "We're gonna get you there."

A wall of forest timber loomed in front of us. There was *no way* we were going to be able to go through that. Certainly we'd have to go around. Yet I could *not* allow myself to miss that train, so I made what, at the time, seemed like a sensible request:

"Can we go any faster?"

Mr. Henderson accelerated and weaved right in.

What followed were ten minutes or ten hours (I couldn't tell which) of terrifying slamming, swerving, and grinding over snow, dirt, and rocks between densely packed trees. Sweat ran down my neck and back. Bile pressed up into my throat. I couldn't breathe, so I didn't scream.

I closed my eyes and flashed on that morning's golf ball–sized snowflakes floating down in a silent, slow-motion dance outside the castle library windows, trapping me in the Colonel's castle.

"Miss Baker, I thought you were leaving us for the day," the Colonel had said as he passed through the room.

I'd pointedly looked outside at the deep snow. "Apparently not."

But two hours later, Mr. Henderson (who was surprisingly hale and chipper for someone recovering from an involuntary effluence experience the night before) showed up driving this snow-racing contraption. Somehow, he had heard of my need to get back to the city to pay my rent. He declared, "There's no such thing as bad weather, only bad vehicles." Accepting his offer of a ride had seemed like a good idea at the time.

My musings took flight when I suddenly became weightless.

Gretchen jumped off a hill crest—the motor whined, my heart beat its wings—and we landed hard on the downhill, fishtailing more or less toward three deer that stared at us as if we were headlights incarnate. Mr. Henderson, his three hundred-plus pounds wedged in behind the wheel, jutted his face forward and gunned it. We veered left and sprayed them with a rooster tail of snow.

I glanced back to see them finally running away. Darwin had smiled upon them today.

Something squawked *boop-boop*. Mr. Henderson touched a button on the wheel. "Talk to me."

The voice of Mr. Haynes burbled through an underwater connection. "The *blub*-tro-North just *blub* Cold Spring."

The train was already at my stop! I'd missed it. Now I was going to be stuck upstate for days. I was going to be evicted from my apartment, my belongings seized. "Shit," I said—which completely failed at expressing my true level of anxiety and despair and anger at the Celestial Spheres for aligning against me. "Fuck!" I said, but that was still inadequate. "Fuck-fuck-fuck!" I really let those Spheres know just how I felt.

"Don't you worry, hon'," Mr. Henderson said. "We're not going to Cold Spring."

"We're not?"

"We're going to Manitou." That was further down the line. Was there still hope? Mr. Henderson boomed, "Haynes, you still there?"

"I *blub*, Mr. Hen-*blub*-son."

"Give me the current ETA to Manitou."

"Elev-*blub*-utes," came the answer.

"We can make that," Mr. Henderson said. "But it's going to be tight."

The motor revved even higher. The trees blurred by.

I glanced at the speedometer—big mistake—and closed my

eyes, prepared to die. There was no point in screaming. We were going to smash into one of those trunks, and that would be it. Some hikers would eventually find our bodies and discover the cash, assume we were drug dealers on the run, and donate the money to their daughter's middle-school orchestra, which would be nice: I'd always wanted to learn how to play cello.

We came to a stop.

I opened my eyes.

We were parked on a high snowbank next to the tracks. Twenty feet away stood a little shelter marked Manitou. It looked more like a bus stop.

"Thank you," I gasped, trying to keep my stomach down.

"Any time. That was fun, wasn't it?" Mr. Henderson said.

I put on a brave smile. "Best cab ride ever."

The door next to me gull-winged up. Fancy. I stuck a nerve-wobbly leg out of Gretchen and climbed out—

—and promptly sank into waist-high snow. "Shit!" The snow was icy, too cold to be very wet—or at all comfortable to someone in a skirt suit.

Through the open door, Mr. Henderson called out, "Sorry about that."

I was only five feet from a cleared walkway. I decided I could just wade through.

"I'm fine. I can walk," I said.

I ended up having to swim. It required all my limbs to make any progress. Over the rumbling idle of Gretchen, I could hear the train coming. *I can't miss the fucking train now!*

Blaaaaaaaaaarrrrrrgh!

Crap! It's nearly here!

Blaaaaaaaaaaaaarrrrrrrgh!

I couldn't tell how far I'd gotten. I kicked my feet and wind-milled my arms, but it felt like the snow was holding me in place. My heart was racing like a hamster in a wheel.

Blaargh!

Shit!

Blaaaaaaaaaaaaoooooooooooooouuuuurrrrrrrrgh!

The engine rolled past. Was it even going to stop?

Suddenly, unexpectedly, I broke through the snow and tum-bled down onto the shoveled walk. I clambered to my feet, gave Mr. Henderson an I-told-you-so smile and wave, and scurried down the ice-packed path as the train slowed to a stop.

2

I STEPPED INTO GRAND CENTRAL precisely one minute after my bank closed. I was going to have to carry ten grand around until the next morning. But I comforted myself with the fact that nobody knew that. As far as anybody was concerned, I was just another New Yorker carrying nothing more than a besieged conscience, a ready temper, and a can of pepper spray. With that in mind, I went ahead to the shiny new ZZZ Midtown Café to wait for Petra, who'd texted that she was on her way.

I was already on my second latte when she entered in the grand, confident manner I'd always secretly envied about her. She wore all black: black coat, black sweater, black leggings, black boots, with a black beret rounding out a nouveau beatnik look. She gave me a half smile and half frown.

I gave a little wave, suddenly feeling guilty. *About what?*

She stepped directly to the barista counter. Two minutes later, she sat across from me with both hands wrapped around her tea, leaned back, and stared into my soul. In her charming Russian accent, she said, "Tell me everything."

And so I told her. I told her about finding the ad for the research job upstate. I told her about the sudden interview invitation. I told her about train ride up the Hudson River Valley sitting next to the smelly little man. I told her about the ginormous castle nestled way back in the woods, far from everything. I told her about the super-rich Colonel who was doing the hiring—but only after he spent a week or two reviewing all the applications, which was nowhere near soon enough.

And I told her about the maid position available immediately, and how I talked this billionaire into hiring me for that.

"As maid," Petra said.

"It's a footman job, really. Footwoman."

"Maid for feet?"

"Not really." I summarized what I'd learned about doing service and how it wasn't anything like what I'd thought. "It's like a dance, where the guests are your partners but you can't let them realize it."

"What kind of guests."

I said, "A whole gaggle of super-rich people who are everything you might expect, only less so."

"The masters," she said, defining the truth—so obvious, she didn't shrug.

"But it's good money."

Now she shrugged. "If given, take it. If beaten, run away."

"Nobody was beating anybody." At least I didn't think so. "Most of the people are nice."

"Most?"

"Well, some, anyway." Truth be told, most of the guests hadn't even noticed me; yet that in itself was a kindness, because it was somehow mortifying for me, as a PhD scholar, to be noticed at all as a mere servant, as a lesser person, as someone beneath consideration as a human being. Invisibility was certainly preferable to the forceful and slobbering attention of Teddy Snoot. "I think they like me."

Petra pulled a knee up under her folded arms and said, "Who could not like you?"

"I don't know. They're all astoundingly rich. They live in a different realm far removed from our world. They are entitled to service. That's their attitude."

"Attitude, feh!" she muttered. This time I got the shrug. "Unhappy people you cannot make happy."

I glanced around to make sure nobody was eavesdropping, and whispered, "They're planning a political campaign."

That actually elicited a raised eyebrow.

I continued, "The Colonel, the man who's running, wants me to spy on his guests because nobody notices the service staff."

"He is colonel of what?" she asked.

That was a good question. "I have no idea. But to convince him I knew my way around politics, I had to name-drop my father."

"And colonel still hire you?"

"Sure. Why not?"

"Your father is with other party."

"How do you know?" I asked.

"I have billion reasons." Then she added, "This job maybe I should have."

She would have been perfect for the job. Politics was her expertise. And she was hot. "You'd look good in the uniform," I said.

"What is uniform?" she asked.

I said, "Short. Fitting. With spiky CFM pumps."

She smirked at me. "This? On you, *malysh*? I must see."

"No!" The thought was far too embarrassing. And, I must confess, exciting. It had been a year and a half since we'd made love. No, I won't bore you with the details.

It felt so good to be back with Petra again, home in the city, with all the noise, with my latte, just hanging. It felt like I hadn't seen her in months, when it had been only two days. "How have you been?"

She looked away, out the window. "Girl break my heart." I could see she was upset but holding it in. "I fall in love, get heart broken, fall out of love." She glanced at me, looked away, glanced at me again, then looked the other way. I knew who she was talking about.

Me.

Okay, so maybe I *should* fill you in on some details. It was our last weekend in our shared university apartment. We were celebrating graduation. We toasted, we drank, we hugged, we kissed, and we ended up making love on the floor among our boxed-up belongings.

That was the one time. Up until then, we had been BFFs. Pals. Chums. Confidantes. And I had never actually slept with any women (a claim nobody seemed to believe). Bisexuality had all been a cerebral, academic, theoretical, and half-virginal concept; but in that moment with Petra, I crossed from the abstract notion into actual physical bisexuality—and what a crossing! It was like I hadn't actually known what sex was before then.

And then the weekend was over. She moved in with her cousin, and I used the last of my student loan money to get my tiny hovel in East Harlem.

We never really sorted out what that weekend meant. It was like we talked past each other—you know, how lovers often do. Blame it on me. I knew I was terrible with romantic relationships, and I didn't want to lose my best friend—especially someone who understood me so well. We always talked about everything, and I mean everything, including those embarrassing things you don't tell anybody, even lovers. And it all was so easy, even when we talked about her other lesbian sexcapades.

And yet after that weekend, my bisexuality was in question because I hadn't dated men for a while. Let's face it: I didn't understand them. (I still don't. They belch. They fart. They pee on the toilet. They are totally lost when it comes to the female body. Some women would say **#notallmen**, that there are in fact some men who are neat and polite and can find your G-spot. I sure hadn't met any—not in *my* bedroom.)

My problem—yes, my *problem*, because it had me a bit confused—was that I still had erotic fantasies about men, but when I met men, I didn't feel any aphrodisia; yet when I met other women, I could find them totally beautiful and sexy, but in my dreams, they usually were not there. So I wasn't quite sure what to say when people asked me: Was I straight? Was I lesbian? People feel more comfortable if they can put you into a box. Which box my box was in? And that left me wondering why, to most people, gay or straight, bi didn't get a box. What made bisexuality so unbelievable to everyone?

Petra would tease me. "Someday, Melody, you must choose. This bisexual stuff is no good. Confusing to others." She'd say that word—bisexual—in a very matter-of-fact way, but to me it was like an ax swinging around, and I always ducked out of instinct.

I'd retort, "Why must I choose?"—which was, I always thought, a rhetorical question. "Can I help whom I'm attracted to?"—which was, I thought, another perfectly adequate rhetorical question.

At that, she would just shrug.

And I would breathe a sigh of relief that we'd avoided talking about *that night.*

Friendship, saved once again.

So now in the café, I looked at her with an open heart. "Petra, I'm not leaving the city."

Her eyes burrowed into me. "You must not."

"It's just a job out of town," I said. I actually believed it at the time. "I just have a bit of a commute."

"In your bones is New York City."

I tried to break her morose mood. "Yeah, but I have expensive bones. I need to work to pay for them."

She looked into her cup and said, "Spent as earned."

"What do you mean by that?" It almost sounded cruel.

She put on a smile. "My tongue is enemy. Speaks ahead of mind." And she shrugged. "You look good." Petra watched me as she sipped her tea. And said nothing. I decided right then that it would be best not to mention Ms. d'Aleu. She wouldn't have understood. I wasn't sure I did. And that left me feeling the need to squirm, so instead, I leaned close and changed the subject.

"I have ten grand in my purse."

That surprised her. "You rob bank without me?"

I told her about how I had so boldly and confidently (ha!) demanded a cash advance as a condition of my taking the maiding job. She nodded with a smile. I let out a huge sigh and said, "I'm no longer broke. That's a big burden off my shoulders. First thing in the morning I'm getting a cashier's check to cover my rent. Then I need to pack some of my stuff. My computer, some clothes."

"But you don't leave us," she said. "You keep apartment."

I gave her what I hoped was a reassuring smile, because it wasn't reassuring me. "I'm not leaving you. Don't worry."

Then Petra dropped a bombshell on me. "Also I have financial opportunity," she said. "I this week fly to District Columbia for interview with think tank."

Heat lanced through my chest. "Is this for a job in Washington?"

"Yes and no," she said. "Much travel. Much thinking."

I thought of her glammed up, flying private jets around the world, meeting with people in fancy restaurants, staying in five-star hotels, and sweeping back into DC to inform the think tank thinkers what to think. It sounded sexy. And far away. I said, "So I'm *not* leaving New York, but you are?"

She said, "I say to them no before three times. But I need H–1B, so this time . . ." She shrugged.

Visa problems? I couldn't bear it if Petra were kicked out of the country permanently. Maybe I'd have to marry her. *Would that be so awful?* I decided not.

I said, "Good luck on the interview. I'm sure you'll be great." And I meant it.

She gave me a dazzling smile. "Of course. They cannot help themselves to with me be impressed." She stood up. "I have again chai. I get you latte?"

3

ITERALLY VIBRATING FROM THE four lattes with Petra, I had trouble swiping my MetroCard at the subway turnstile. As I skipped down the stairs, passing below the noise of the streets and the rushing water running down storm drains and subway vents, the damp heat and sour smell of the tunnels hit me full on. The stench felt like a warm embrace. The screeching, rattling subway trains sang to me as they passed by, welcoming me back from my adventures in faraway lands.

Upon boarding, I took a corner seat. Then I waited as we rumbled uptown, pausing at each and every station, people getting on and off, doors bing-bonging.

It seemed like forever before we reached my stop. The cold

evening air refreshingly stung my face as I climbed the stairs
to 110th Street.

In Manhattan, I love the snow. It blankets the city in quiet.
Bright white covers the grime and garbage, at least for a few
hours. And everyone bundles up, and somehow that translates
into people not getting up into one another's faces so much.
It's like we all mellow out a bit when there's fresh snow on the
ground.

That did not mean I could be complacent. Just what I needed
was someone to snatch my purse and all that cash. So I hugged
my bag like a child as I marched down the block, wearing my
don't-fuck-with-me face while visualizing what I was going to
do to get my life in order: pay my rent, get some clothes, eat
some sushi, hang with Petra. As I walked toward my apartment,
the familiar apartment buildings, the local stores, my local pizza
joint, my local deli all brought up a welling sense of nostalgia—
which was silly. I had to remind myself I'd been gone only a day.

The eviction notice taped to my door greeted me as I reached
my landing, but in my well-funded mood, I saw only bureau-
cratic poetry:

> *Pay the amount above*
> *Within three days*
> *Or forfeit said premises*
> *And all contents within.*

It ended with the lovely couplet:

> *Payment must be made by money order*
> *Or cashier's check, by court order.*

I ripped that missive down. The tape took some paint layers
with it, leaving exposed an ancient green undercoat. Something

else for the landlord to ding me for. I folded up the notice and shoved it into my purse. *Tomorrow morning, I'll hand it to Kakkas with my goddam certified check.*

My apartment greeted me with a ninety-degree sauna treatment, thanks to my radiator run amok. I threw open the window. Cold, damp air wafted in from the alley, mixing the scent of damp soot with burning dust. Using the ratty washcloth on the floor next to the radiator, I gave the valve a few quick turns to cut off the steam. Now my apartment would reach a comfortable temperature—eventually.

I poured myself a glass of water and guzzled it. I poured myself another, set it by my bed, and flopped down, exhausted.

But I couldn't sleep.

Every time I started to drift off, I snapped awake, certain that the money was gone. But of course it was still there, tucked in my purse.

I pulled the wad out. I couldn't stop myself from smelling that stack. Do a hundred $100 bills smell different than a hundred ones? It sure seemed like it. There's nothing like the smell of cash, especially when it's the most cash you've held in your hands at one time. It smells like victory. Or a dusty basement. Right then, ten thousand dollars in cash smelled like I would be able to keep this apartment—which smells nice on most days. (Lavender oil is the trick.)

I stashed the cash under my pillow to ensure it wouldn't walk away. But then the thick lump under the clumped feathers prevented me from drifting off. There was just no sleeping with that much cash.

And so I lay there on the bed, reflecting on the past thirty-six

hours—from unemployed PhD to employed maid-cum-spy—
and tried to will away the knot in my stomach. Though maiding
provided a reprieve from privation, I knew deep down that I
belonged at a university, teaching bright minds about language
and writing and critical thinking and rhetoric. I pictured myself in Cambridge or Hyde Park or Berkeley or Morningside
Heights, where I'd assign short essays to freshmen, teaching
them the basics of structure and the methods of ethos, pathos,
and logos. For sophomores, I'd assign three longer papers and
have them submit revisions at least three times each so they'd
learn the value of rewriting. For the upper division, it would be
term papers from week one, with readings on Booth, Foucault,
Barthes, and of course Derrida. I'd have an office in an old
building with a window facing campus, and a desk and a couch,
and I'd put up prints of old movie posters, just to irritate the
other faculty, and I'd have office hours all day when I wasn't in
class, and host sherry hours and invite people who were top in
their field to talk about their passions and ideals and methods.
It would be grand.

I awoke with a start, sweating and shivering on top of the
covers. An icy wind had brought the apartment down to a definitely not-hot thirty degrees Fahrenheit. Still half-asleep, I
jumped up and slammed shut the window, then leapt back into
bed, drawing the covers over me.

I could feel that the lump of cash was still there under my
head. My phone read 7:47 AM. Morning daylight refracted gold
and blue through the frozen glass of water by my bed, hinting
at clear skies and sunshine. Hope and joy flooded into me—but
it wasn't keeping me warm. I wanted to just go to the café and

warm up with a nice hot latte, but I was a bit afraid to do it with ten grand in my bag. This cash was becoming a real pain in the ass. I had to cover my rent and get on with living.

At least that was the plan.

4

I SHOWERED, DRESSED IN MY New York business casual look—white Façconable blouse, black wool Anne Klein pencil skirt, and (in my appreciation of foot comfort) my black Ecco knee-high boots—and finished the look off with my lucky pilcrow earrings (which I had retrieved from Ms. Metz the day before), my silver necklace with the triangle pendant Petra had given to me for my birthday, and a simple ox-horn barrette to pull back my hair. I stepped out of my building feeling good, hopeful, powerful.

My spirits sagged just a tad upon discovering the mass of people at my bank branch just a few blocks uptown from my apartment. The tiny interior—which was actually smaller than my apartment—provided for a crowded wait in line behind the twenty-seven people who apparently had greater banking ambitions than I. We all stood, waiting to be served by one of the two bomb-proof-glass-encased tellers.

Lest you get the wrong impression, I should tell you that my bank embraces nothing but the highest corporate ideals: they charge fees for everything from writing a check to accessing your balance; they diligently cut expenses at every level, from workers' salaries to the amount of ink loaded into the lobby pens; and they excel at managing the customer as a nothing more than another problem to be solved. My bank's idea of customer service is to provide a place for you to wait and wait and wait until you give up and try to make do at the ATM (which is out of service half the time).

I couldn't resort to that option. Thank the stars I'd decided to wear my flat-heeled boots because it took a good forty-nine minutes to move up in line and finally step up to the teller, a young blond man who looked old enough for tenth grade, if that.

"Good morning," his reedy voice squeaked through a tinny little speaker apparently repurposed from a 1965 transistor radio. "Beautiful day, isn't it?" The pimples covering his baby-fat cheeks undulated as he spoke.

"I need to make a deposit," I said.

"ID, deposit slip, and endorsed check,"

"I'm depositing cash."

"Sorry, we don't accept cash," he said.

"What?" That made absolutely no sense. "But I have an account here."

"We thank you for your patronage."

"This *is* a bank, isn't it?" I asked pointedly.

"Yes."

"So I want to deposit some cash."

"We do not accept cash deposits."

"Banks are where people put their money." It's possible that my voice started to rise just a bit.

"Yes."

"I need to deposit money into my account."

"I am here to assist you, ma'am," he said in a blandly pleasant way. *Ma'am!*

"Great. So if you slide out the pass-through drawer here, I'll give you the cash, and you can count it and credit my account, and then you can give me a cashier's check made out to—"

"I'm sorry, we are unable to issue cashier's checks at this time."

I looked at him. "Why not?"

"The check printer is out of paper," he said—as if that was a real answer.

"So make one out by hand," I said.

He said, "I'm sorry, only managers are permitted to issue hand-drawn cashier's checks."

"So have a manager write up the check," I said.

"We don't have a manager at this branch," he said.

"Of course you have a manager. Every branch has a branch manager!"

"Our regional trunk manager is located off-site," he intoned, then shifted his voice into friendly mode to add, "You may speak to our manager using our complimentary courtesy phone conveniently located at the back of the lobby." (See what I mean about my bank's exceptional corporate values?)

"Fine," I said. "What about money orders?"

"We issue money orders," he said.

Great. "So I would like you to draw up a money order, and I will give you the cash to cover it."

"This branch does not accept cash."

"I don't want to deposit cash. I just want to give you cash to cover the money order."

"This branch does not accept cash, ma'am."

"What *do* you handle? Monopoly money?"

He blithely responded, "We accept checks, money orders, traveler's checks, wire transfers, and Bitcoin."

"Wait. You accept Bitcoin, which isn't even real money, but you won't accept cash?"

"That is correct, ma'am," the boy teller said.

My blood pressure was rising. I could feel the vein in my forehead starting to throb. "So how am I supposed to deposit money into my account?"

"I mean, I can assist you with your deposit. But we do not handle cash at this branch."

This was going horribly. I could feel myself getting flush. Tears were welling in my eyes, threatening to trickle down my face in a genuine expression of pathos. "Why not?"

"It's policy."

"What kind of policy is that?"

The boy teller's eyes flitted down to something below the blast shield. "Ma'am, if you have no business to transact, please step aside. Other customers are waiting."

"I have business to transact, but you are refusing to transact it."

The tow-headed weasel actually grimaced at me. "No cash deposits are accepted at this branch."

"What kind of bank doesn't do money transactions?" I glared at him with the hardest glare I could muster, but its effect must have been attenuated by the glass because he did not appear to be at all impressed—let alone intimidated. The bravery of small men out of reach of consequences.

"Please step aside, ma'am."

I'd had enough. "I'd like to speak with your manager."

The boy teller said, "Certainly. You may speak to our regional trunk manager via our complimentary courtesy phone conveniently located at the back of the lobby."

How did my beautiful morning of potential become such a Kafkaesque nightmare? I took a deep breath to calm myself. When that didn't work, I counted to ten to calm myself. When that didn't work, I decided I didn't need to be calm. "So"—*you fucking little twerp*—"which branch *can* take my cash and give me a cashier's check?"

He smiled as if suddenly understanding a question that had been confusing him. "Water Street branch."

"Water Street?"

For you non-New Yorkers, that is way the fuck downtown—as in the Wall Street area, miles away, where misery and tears are optioned for profit.

"Yes, ma'am," the boy teller said, "the Water Street branch can handle all your cash transactions."

I glared at him. He gazed back at me with the dead, bureaucrat eyes of a fifty-year-old. "Thank you," I said. "You'll go far in banking."

"Thank you, ma'am."

5

NEW YORK CITY IS a pressure cooker. It presses in from all sides. You have to be able to escape, or at least slip out of the way, every now and then. Otherwise you wind up a ground-down slug. Or you pop.

You can see the popped New Yorkers every day: They're the ones loping around in barely suppressed rage. Their armor—all of us New Yorkers develop armor—has been pierced somehow, and they're hurting, waving metaphorical swords to keep people at bay. Even their laughter has an angry, maniacal edge to it. If you see someone who's popped, keep your distance, and by all means avoid eye contact. They can spot you from five blocks away.

Yet for all the popped people, they're outnumbered tenfold by the grinders—the people who've just been taking it, and taking it, and taking it, and bending a little bit each time, each year, with each blow, each indignity, until they're permanently bent. You see them hunched over, walking like bipedal turtles with their heads retracted but still going forward. Even on this day when the threatened back-to-back nor'easters failed to arrive and patches of blue passed overhead, the grinders didn't notice. Or they didn't care. Comfort can get uncomfortable when discomfort dominates your comfort zone.

When I stepped out of the bank, I wasn't sure if I was popped or ground down. I didn't care. If I started yelling at people, well, then I'd know. So I hunched over and glared at everybody and anybody who dared even glance at me. I was a mama hyena ready to tear apart anyone who dared approach my ten-thousand-dollar cub in the bottom of my bag. I now had to go all the way to Wall Street to accomplish my mission. I drew up my defense shields, cast my eyes at the sidewalk, and stormed toward the subway.

The day may have been sunny, but the storm had left its residue. Pedestrians had to maneuver around piles of slush on the sidewalks, along the curbs, and in every intersection. Men and women scurried along, hunched over against the wind that wasn't there, huddled against potential assaults and indignities. A few raged at life's injustice. One distraught elderly man fulminated at length at an empty storefront, as if the rusted metal roll-down gate could hear him. Another strutted in the middle of Lexington Avenue, waving a Bible as he damned any and all of us for consuming pasteurized milk. One man in a slick suit grumbled with assessments of people as they walked by: "*You* don't watch television. *You* don't watch television. *You* don't watch *enough* television. *You* watch, but I bet you skip the commercials. The commercials are what matter, you selfish jerks!"

And these popped people were minor league. The big-shot ranters took over corners on 57th Street in Midtown, where they could cow the shoppers from Long Island and Connecticut and downright frighten the tourists.

As I reached my block, I saw a cube truck, tailgate open, double-parked in front of my building. In the back I saw a table and chairs that looked like mine. Someone had good taste.

Then I did a double-take. Those *were* my table and chairs! An eel started twisting around in my stomach.

I ran into my building and bounded up the stairs just as two lunks were coming down carrying a dresser.

My dresser!

"That's mine!" I shouted. "What are you doing?" I tried to block their way, but the lunk in the lead was just too big. He pushed past me like I was a curtain. Or a door—a door without a stopper because I slammed against the wall. My heart was racing. Despite the cold, these men were wearing tank tops and were all sweaty.

"Sorry," the second lunk said, and he babbled something else—I couldn't tell what. It sounded like what a parrot would say in its native parrot language. *Edo eka kana peepeezoopoo.* Something like that. It sure as hell wasn't English or Pig Latin. I was stumped.

I dug my phone out and snapped a picture of them as they rounded the corner of the landing.

The second lunk grinned at me, flashing gold caps. Words sounding like *epitepimoo napeepeezoo stissass* came out of his mouth, and the first guy practically sang *eye-na my zoola*.

"Eye-na my zoola yourself, assholes!" I shouted—whatever that meant—and raced up the stairs to my apartment.

The door was ajar, with a new bright yellow notice taped to it:

EVICTION NOTICE: THESE PREMISES SUBJECT TO IMMEDIATE SEIZURE BY LANDLORD.

Fuck!

I pushed open the door and looked inside, and right then my heart stopped and despair erupted from my chest.

My studio was stripped bare. All the furniture was gone. Pictures, gone. Books, gone. Rug, gone. Remnants of my clothes, piled on the floor. Papers, scattered everywhere. Dust bunnies, dead in the corners.

And my computer was missing. *All my work. My files! My programs!* My life was destroyed!

The rational voice in my head reminded me that I had all my files backed up in the cloud, and the laptop itself was six years old, yet that didn't help. I felt violated.

I walked inside. My closet was empty. The kitchenette had been cleaned out of everything, including my All-Clad omelet pan. My cookbook collection was missing, too. *Fuckers.*

I turned to the small pile of clothes: a couple of old sundresses; my favorite Queens of the Stone Age shirt that had the tear in the front from where it got hooked on a wrought-iron fence the summer before last; skinny jeans that never quite fit over my butt; fugly yellow capris I don't remember buying; and the two pair of striped orange emergency undies—my do-the-laundry motivation. Everything of value was taken. All I had were the clothes on my back and what lay at my feet.

At that point, I launched into a loud and colorful tirade that made up with foul language what it lacked in eloquence. It lasted a good thirty seconds, and would have gone longer if I hadn't started sobbing. I grabbed my QOTSA T-shirt to blubber into.

All right, I told myself. *Don't panic. You have the cash. You can pay Kakkas cash for your rent, and then have the lunks carry your stuff back up to the apartment. Money greases the wheels.*

I hurried down the stairs to the landlord's apartment.

6

AFTER NOT EVEN TWO seconds of my pounding on the door of 1B, Mr. Kakkas, the landlord, yanked it open as if he'd been waiting for me. He sneered. His too-tight white tank top and blue-and-white briefs displayed way too much of his pale, skinny, lumpy, hairy body.

"What?"

"Mr. Kakkas," I said. "I can pay my rent now. I got a job—"

"Too late," he said in a flat voice.

"I can pay you right now. All of it."

He waved his hand and said something like *ochee*. It sounded like no.

"You have to take it," I said. "I have cash."

At that, his entire demeanor changed. His mustache spread wide over his closed-mouth smile. He said, "Good."

Good!

He watched while I pulled out the envelope of cash and started counting out hundreds.

I said, "So three months is—"

"Four months," he said.

I was so flustered, I just said, "Right, okay," and started counting out the hundred-dollar bills. "One, two . . . five . . . then. Eleven . . . fifteen . . . twenty."

He said nothing as I whispered my tally. "Fifty. That's five thousand. And one . . . five . . . six thousand . . . five . . . and seven thousand . . . five . . . eight thousand . . ."

That fat stack of security was getting pretty thin. But four months of rent added up to nine thousand eight hundred eighty dollars. I peeled off the last of ninety-nine hundreds, leaving me with one, and handed the stack over. "So I get twenty back," I said.

He folded the bills and tucked the wad into the back of his briefs. He made no indication that he was going to give me any change.

"Okay, so we'll count it against the next month," I said. "So could you please have the movers bring my stuff back in?"

"Too late."

"I'll pay for their time."

"You are out. Evicted! Someone else signed the lease. Moves in tomorrow."

No! That's not fair! He just accepted my rent money! But I couldn't just rage at him. I had to be diplomatic. Get him on my side.

So I smiled and said, trying to keep the anger out of my voice, "Mr. Kakkas, I've lived here almost two years—"

"You stop paying rent. What am I supposed to do? I have a building to run. You're out! Find another place."

"But this is my place! I paid you all my rent! You can't just take my stuff and kick me out!"

He regarded me with narrowed eyes. "Thank you for paying what you owed."

He closed the door in my face.

I was stunned. I pounded on the door. "Then you owe me my security deposit!"

Silence.

I pounded some more, but he didn't answer. I yelled some of my choicest epithets at him. I'm sure I really hurt his feelings.

But I couldn't dwell on that.

I had to stop the movers from leaving with all my stuff.

7

EVERYTHING SEEMED TO HAPPEN in slow motion: I lurched up the hallway toward the building's front door. My back foot slipped. I stumbled, caught myself with a hand on the floor. My purse hit me in the head. I bounced off the mailboxes just inside the lobby. My arm extended, I shoved the door—which was latched. My shoulder slammed into the doorframe. I squeezed the door latch. The door flung open, sending me stumbling outside and down the stoop to land on the sidewalk. I scrambled to my feet. Sunlight glared in my eyes.

There was no sign of any moving truck.

At first I just stood there, numb.

My mood darkened as my new reality set in. My plan to

settle up my rent had exploded in my face. I had no home, no belongings—nothing but the clothes on my back, a one-hundred-dollar bill, and forty-three cents. My rescue cash was gone. Stolen! I was adrift. My lifelong dream of academia was out of reach. I was evicted not just from my apartment but from my life. Panic began to bubble up into my throat.

I would have started hyperventilating, but right then a large chemical-tanker truck with *Molten Sulfur* painted on the side roared by right in front of me, its tires kicking up an eight-foot wall of oily slushy muck, drenching me head to foot.

I lost my breath as the chill cut me to the bone. My coat was open, so I was soaked not just on my hair, face and neck, and legs and feet, but also on my chest and breasts and waist and thighs—soaked with a frozen muddy stew of road filth, oil, soot, and New York City garbage.

The Spheres were definitely conspiring to compel me to leave.

I wiped my face with my QOTSA T-shirt. *What now?* I didn't know. I started for the subway.

At first I intended to head down to Astor Place and go by Petra's. But then the sinking truth that she was out of town sucked the last of my hope away. I was alone.

A vindictive wind rushing down East 96th blasted away any hint of resistance against my virtuous self-pity as I fought my way up to Lex. My brain disassociated from the bitter-cold piercing every inch of my skin by skittering around in search of Reasons for my suffering: payback for mocking those souls earlier who'd been hunkered down against weather (*they knew, they knew!*); bad karma for my outburst at the bank teller (*the twerp*); retribution for having gone for the maid job cash instead of sticking to my dreams (*my bourgeois failings*).

I started to shiver even as my legs ached from the climb up the hill. I practically charged right into a couple of phone-focused high school girls who giraffed on their spiky platform shoes across the snow-packed sidewalk right into my path.

I gave them a scolding glare. Startled, they winced at me—not as in *Oh, poor girl, you got all wet*, but rather as in *Oh, how disgusting to have to look at you all covered with muck!* I sneered right back at them and clomped down the stairs into the warm, fragrant humidity of the subway station.

On the platform, catching my breath, I zoned out, running what-if scenarios through my head: What if I had just skipped the bank in the first place and paid my back rent first thing in the morning? What if I had paid cash the day before? What if I'd had my checking account at a bank that actually handles cash? What if I knew kung fu and kicked Mr. Kakkas's ass? What if I shoved a rug full of bedbugs under Mr. Kakkas's door? Or a snake? A snake for a snake. What if—

Subway doors opened in front of me. I hadn't even noticed the train's arrival. I shuffled in and collapsed onto a seat. The doors bing-bonged closed.

At each station, people got on; some glanced at me, but most did not, and those who did didn't linger, leaving me alone to my own particular misery. New Yorkers understand this shit. At times, we can be quite decent people.

I sat there, not moving, not really thinking about anything except that stop by stop I was rolling away from my neighborhood that was no longer my neighborhood, toward what was,

I had believed, a temporary job but in actual fact was appearing to be my new career—at least until Election Day.

The train car flooded with light as we emerged from the tunnels, and I realized that at some point I had reached Grand Central Station and gotten onto the Metro North. I didn't remember any of it—boarding, or being in Grand Central, or even getting off the subway. Zombie me had been in charge, taking me away from my evicted life.

Harlem slid by.

The Palisades across the Hudson slid by.

Red construction cranes slid by.

The train rocked a bit as the Croton rail yard crawled by.

The bluffs at Peekskill slid by.

Dobbs Ferry slid by.

Snow-flocked evergreens and sprouting spring leaves were everywhere.

I was sitting facing backward. No career, no home, exiled from the city up into my own private Siberia in the boonies, far away from all that I knew, including my one and only best friend, my life was now thoroughly deconstructed.

I pulled out my phone and saw a text from Petra timestamped two hours before:

> *interview resched where r u? get*
> *dinner i know party after*

Petra! I could have gone to her and cried on her shoulder. She would have given me some pithy wisdom to feel better. Something like, *Money makes you target. Poverty keeps you safe.* Which of course is not pithy—it doesn't even make sense. But would probably have made me feel better.

I tapped out a reply:

> My life sucks. I lost my apartment and
> must live in exile. Don't try to follow.
> Save yourself! I will send a message via
> carrier pigeon when I can.

When I touched send, the progress bar of frustration appeared at the top of my screen. I had no signal. A few moments later, I got *Service Unavailable*. I was about to try again when my screen went black. It was out of power.

Powerless.

8

THE CAB RIDE UP from the station took over an hour as the Chevy Suburban negotiated the slushy roads that had been driven on but not plowed. The driver, a grizzled old guy wearing a roadster cap, tried to strike up conversation. "Beautiful day, ain't it?"

I just stared out the window, trying to identify animals to keep my mind off of things. *Oh, there's a squirrel. There's another squirrel. There's a bird. What kind of bird? A brown bird. Oh, that bird is speckled. There's a red bird. I know that kind: a cardinal!* I was practically an ornithologist.

The main gate to the Colonel's estate was wide open with many heavy tire tracks through the snow. As we headed up the driveway, I thought I saw someone with a machine gun. Too much vengeance on my mind. I was seeing things.

In front of the castle were a long black van and a large semi with a trailer equipped with numerous open side bins. Things were already happening.

As the cab pulled up to the castle's portico, I saw a man in black lurking in the bushes off to the side. Was that a worker? No. He was dressed in all black with a black mask. What was he? Some kind of prowler after the Colonel? A spy for the opposition? Whatever it was, I didn't like the look of him. I started to feel a knot in my stomach. For safety, I needed to be dropped closer to the service entrance on the east side of the building.

"Could you drive up to the corner of the building there?" I asked the driver.

"Sure thing," he said. The taxi drove forward the thirty or so yards. I gave him the last of my cash to cover the meter, shoved the door open, and quickly walked up the east side of the castle.

I heard footsteps behind me. Someone was following me.

My sensible heels kept slipping on the ice as I skittered along.

"Hey!" the man shouted. "Stop!"

I ran.

But the man gained on me.

"Help!" I screamed. "Help me!"

Something heavy slammed into my back. I flung out my hands as the ice-encrusted ground flew up at me, hitting me hard.

A knee pressed into my spine. "Got you," the man said and yanked my arms back. Cold metal wrapped around my wrists and tightened with ratchet clicks.

He flung me onto my back. He was about thirty-five and chubby—which, I'm afraid, speaks volumes about how slow I must have been for him to be able to catch me. He ripped off his black mask, revealing a ruddy face flushed pink with rage. Obviously he was one of the men in the world who have problems managing their adrenaline and testosterone. Men in this state are easily frightened. I lay completely still and limp.

"WHO ELSE IS THERE?" he bellowed into my face.

I shook my head. What was he? Some kind of security guard?

"WHO ELSE CAME WITH YOU?"

"The cab driver?"

"HE'S BEING QUESTIONED NOW, SO TELL ME THE TRUTH! WHO BESIDES YOU?"

This was starting to get a little frightening. I was concerned that this guy might hit me—or have a stroke and leave me pinned under his three hundred fifty pounds. I said in my little meek voice, "It's just me."

"BULLSHIT! WHO THE FUCK ELSE IS THERE?"

"Nobody—"

"WHO ARE YOU? YOU'RE IN A RESTRICTED AREA! YOU KNOW WHAT WE DO TO PEOPLE WHO TRESPASS?"

Now I definitely had difficulty breathing. "I work here."

"BULLSHIT! WHERE'S YOUR PASS?"

"What pass?"

"WHAT ARE YOU AFTER?"

Now I was scared into yelling back, "I said I work here, you dumbshit!"

He glared at me, huffing and puffing. His eyes softened. His color subsided. In a gentle voice, he said, "Okay," and he stood up. "But you oughta have a pass."

I somehow scrambled to my feet without use of my arms. "Who the hell are you?"

The thug put up a pudgy hand. "Easy, honey."

I stepped toward him. Not an advised moved, but I was pissed. "I'm not your honey."

"I'm just doing my job."

"Your job is to assault innocent women?"

That got his attention. He sneered, "How do I know you're not a terrorist?"

I sneered right back, "How do I know you're not a rapist?"

He shook his head. "Hey, I didn't touch you. Not like that."

"Like what? Like knocking me down? Hurting me? Look at my knee!" My sore knee was throbbing again. For a moment, I wondered whether Ms. d'Aleu was around to administer more first aid.

He whined, "But you don't have a pass! I was just doing my job."

I shouted, "You're not letting me do mine. You idiot!"

He took a step back.

I pressed forward. "It's a shitty job, but I signed up for it, and I'm here, and what do you do? You attack me and handcuff me!"

"But—" he said.

"I just lost my home because of this job!" Yeah, not quite the cause and effect, but he didn't know that, and I was going for effect. I think my tears helped. "I lost everything I had! My apartment, my stuff, my clothes, my favorite PJs. I'm exiled from the city. This castle is the closest thing I have to a home now. And what happens when I come back here? You and your cretinous idea —"

"Hippo-dog," a deep voice said, "looks like you caught something."

A handlebar-mustachioed man nearly as big as the belligerent blockhead leaned against the outer wall of the castle. And like the belligerent blockhead, he wore close-cropped hair, a radio earpiece, and black body armor. And a pistol was strapped to his belt.

"I'm not a *something*," I snapped at him. "I'm a footman!"

"A what?"

"A footman," I said, and added, "A footwoman, actually."

His handlebar mustache twitched. "You like feet?"

"What? No." I took a deep breath to calm myself. "I work for the Colonel. I'm on the service staff."

"So . . . what, you give foot massages? Count me in." He grinned.

I leveled at him my are-you-fucking-kidding-me stare and said, "Another name for it is 'parlor maid.'"

He frowned and touched his earpiece, listening. Then he looked at me and laughed. That's right, he laughed! At me! "The cab driver checks out. You don't seem to be much of a threat. Hippo-dog, release her."

"Yes, Boss," the belligerent blockhead Hippo-dog said. I felt a tug on my wrists, and I was freed. I rubbed the angry red welts. I glared at Hippo-dog. I glared at handlebar mustache.

He gazed up at the sky. "Beautiful day, isn't it?"

What's so beautiful about it?

"What's your name, miss?" handlebar mustache said.

"Melody Baker." *Miss Baker. Dr. Baker.*

He scrolled through something on a tablet. "Yes, there you are. You missed the security briefing this morning."

"I was otherwise occupied," I said.

"You need to come with me."

"I have to change first."

"No privileges until you've completed the security briefing."

9

HE LED ME THROUGH the kitchen into an anteroom more spacious than my former apartment. Inside, along the wall, stood eleven other hulking brutes larger than your average non-human-growth-hormone-fed *Homo sapiens*, who also wore buzz cuts, radio earpieces, black body armor, and holstered sidearms. Several had visible tattoos on their necks and hands. They all squared off to face me. I think they meant to appear intimidating, like paramilitary riot police, but they looked more like extras from a dystopian sci-fi movie.

In an announcerly voice with a deliberately semi-bored, metered cadence, no doubt to impress me with his old-hand experience, handlebar mustache announced, as if there were a dozen of me in the room, "My name is Spiro Arkady. You can call me Sparky. I am in charge of special security for the Colonel, his staff, and his estate during his campaign for the Senate."

I said, "Hello, Sparky," which seemed to throw him off.

He began to pace, arms hanging wide in that macho demeanor you always see with men who have a slightly unhealthy fetish for their own authority. "I and my associates," he said loudly, "are working to transition all operations to a full-ready status to ensure that comprehensive, vigorous, and vigilant security is maintained at all times."

I noticed that two of these security men were actually women. They looked just as tough, with the same no-bullshit expressions, the same linebacker physiques, but without the five-o'clock shadows. One of the women, with light brown skin and a nose ring, met my gaze and held it, and I felt like she was seeing right into my quailing insides.

Did she just wink at me?

Sparky raised his voice even more. "Access and Egress."

He said it like that, with capital letters, as if it was a heading in his speech.

"The entire estate, as of this moment, is under twenty-four-hour monitoring and control. You will be issued a personal color-coded identification pass with an encrypted microchip that at any point in time can identify you, your position, and which areas of the estate you have business in."

I asked, "Are we going to get those cute little flag pins to wear on our lapels, too?"

He sighed. "Wear your pass at all times. Every time you enter the compound or leave the compound, or enter or leave the building, or move from one sector of the building to another, you must submit to ID check."

I thought about how an ID check might have affected my assisting Mr. Henderson the other night. Probably not good. "What if I need to go to the bathroom?"

Sparky planted his feet and folded his arms and glared at me. "Now, over the next few days, you'll see us everywhere, sometimes getting in your way. I'm afraid that's unavoidable. But within a week, you'll hardly notice us. When the Colonel is on the road campaigning, we will have people with his entourage and here on the premises. Any questions so far?"

He threw down those last four words like a challenge. He didn't want to hear questions. I shook my head.

"We Are Armed," he said.

"That explains the machine gun guy," I said. He glared at me again. I guessed I wasn't supposed to interrupt. I tried to explain. "I saw him outside as we drove in."

Sparky took a moment to bite his lip. "You were supposed to notice," he said.

I wasn't buying it, but whatever.

He resumed his speechifying. "Every one of my team members is trained in hand-to-hand combat, light and heavy weaponry, military and guerrilla methods, counterterrorism measures, armor and infantry tactics, and crowd control. We are prepared to meet any threat, any incursion, with deadly force."

"You really think it would come to that?" I asked. My father never faced anything close to deadly force, and he'd been in Congress for over twenty years.

Sparky chose to ignore me and resumed pacing. "Now. If You Notice Anything Unusual. Maybe you look out the window and see a strange man with a gun. It's imperative that you just act natural."

I said, "Pay no attention to the strange man with the gun."

Sparky really glared at me—this time some serious glaring, as if I were heckling a church sermon. "Make note of what details you can without altering your routine. And notify any one of my associates. We will address any situation from there."

"Right," I said, "ignore the sniper and just serve tea."

Sparky sighed. "If We Are in a Situation." He stepped close. I immediately felt cold. "It is imperative that you follow our instructions without hesitation. I don't want to have someone questioning why they should hit the deck or crawl behind a wall. You'll end up getting us both killed. I don't tell you this to alarm you. If a problem occurs, don't you worry. We know what we're doing. We are experienced experts. We get into fights two or three times a week."

I felt safer already.

10

As I stepped back into the kitchen with my brand-spanking-new Blue Pass, Ms. Metz blocked my path and took in my wet, muddy, scraped-up appearance. "What happened to you on such a beautiful day?"

I must have looked like a subway rat. I thought of trying to explain, but what could I say? "Security briefing."

Ms. Metz shook her head. "When you're off duty, you are to stay in the service area." She tipped her head to get my full attention. "Are you off duty?"

I forced a smile. "I just got back." I waved my pass. "I'm official now."

"Uniform is required at all times when on duty."

Great. "Understood."

"Supper at four."

I nodded.

"Curtsy."

My curtsy muscles ached. My injured knee ached. My whole body ached. And everything ached all the more as I climbed the stairs to the fourth-floor servants' level.

I stepped into the Athena room, which now comprised my entire world, or what was left of it. How appropriate—a bare room with a twin bed, a narrow dresser, and no windows.

Someone had left some folded towels on the bed. How thoughtful. Actually, one of the towels was a robe. That was all the urging I needed. I stripped off my muddy clothes and undies then pulled on the robe. What was I going to do about underwear? I stuffed my panties and bra into the robe pocket and, just in case, slipped my Blue Pass lanyard over my head.

At the end of the hall I found a bathroom so old it was classic. I might have squeed with delight over the giant vintage clawfoot tub, the pedestal sink with brass fittings, and the toilet with an overhead tank—if they didn't remind me that I had no apartment, no home to call my own.

Thankfully the tub had a hose nozzle. If I had to take a bath at that point, I'd have never gotten out. I'd have just soaked until I dissolved away, and people would have wondered, *What happened to Miss Baker?* And the only clue would have been the ring of despair sediment around the tub. I showered, using whatever was in the bottle there as a body wash. It smelled like strawberries. The hot water felt fantastic. I actually started to feel not miserable. The stream drenched my hair, rinsing out the

Manhattan mud. I was a new woman. A new upstate woman, anyway.

After drying off, I washed my panties and bra in the sink. When I got back to my room, I draped them on the radiator, which was barely warm. They were going to take some time to dry.

I sat on the bed and considered that it was actually kind of nice to have a radiator that functioned properly. The room was warm without being Death Valley hot. Maybe getting out of that apartment wasn't all bad. It had never really felt like home anyway—not like the apartment I'd shared with Petra.

Petra.

For all of two seconds I considered asking Petra if I could crash with her and her cousin. But they shared a one-hundred-square-foot studio—barely a closet, even by my standards.

What I really need to do is figure out what to do now.

I couldn't hunt for another apartment, not until I had money again. And my computer. And my books. And my clothes.

Kakkas, that thief! I wanted to go back there and do something really mean to him, like break his dishes. Maybe I could borrow one of Ms. d'Aleu's guns and scare him. Maybe I could borrow Ms. d'Aleu, and *she* could scare him.

What else could I do? Make use of the New York City safety net? Stay at a shelter? *Ha! Far too dangerous.* And I was convinced that finding a box to set up in front of an office building wouldn't have worked. Good boxes were hard to come by, and all the best places were probably taken.

Dancing at Skoochy's would pay cash in hand—or rather tucked under a g-string. But can I really do that? Baring my breasts and writhing around in front of a bunch of mouth-breathing men? Even worse, what if I proved to have pole-dancing talent and get dependent on the money and can't quit? What if I become famous? (Of course I'd have to have a stage name. Something like Trixie the Vixie.) What if I get recognized? And someone videos me and puts it up on YouTube? Congressman's Daughter Exposed! PhD Bares Bosom! My father would explode.

I certainly couldn't go running back to my parents. They had their hands full with my porn-addled little brother who was living in my parent's downsized-house guest room. Reed had studied art in college but dropped out to pursue a career as an airbrush painter at a surf shop. I shouldn't call him an actual loser. After all, he paints the best alien monsters on the whole south coast. One time a Newport gallery even did a show for him, hanging surfboards and skateboards he'd airbrushed with planets, sharks, spiders, and snakes. They even displayed the hood of a Firebird covered with dragons. That night he sold seven surfboards at twelve hundred dollars a pop. But averaged out over the year, he wasn't making much of a living, and as bad off as I was in my maid-or-street predicament, I couldn't bear the thought of swapping places with him.

I was supposed to be setting the example. I was supposed to be the wise owl, not the flightless turkey. There was no way I, penniless and careerless, could face my father—not after he spent years (*years!*) browbeating me to go to law school. Did I mention that he called getting a PhD in English a *pipe dream?* Did you know he had been calling me every Sunday for the past year just to ask whether I'd gotten a teaching job yet? Did I tell you that the last time I borrowed money from him, he took it as license to audit what I was eating, how I was spending every minute of the day, how much my electricity bill was running, everything? Not that I was frivolous in any of those areas, but it's something else to live under constant surveillance. He treated me like he had hired me as his daughter, and that pay was well below minimum wage.

That was back in college, and I never borrowed anything from him since. Not that my parents couldn't afford it. After all, he was a sitting Congressman, and we all know how Congress manages to attend to their own salaries, even if they ignore pay increases for anyone else. And my mother made beaucoup bucks as a civil rights attorney in Orange County—that is, when she won a settlement, which was every few years.

Take my word for it. I, the prodigal daughter of lawyers, had to figure this out myself.

I stood there in the middle of the room, looking at the only decoration—the comedy-tragedy masks on the wall that had mocked me two nights before. I looked from one face to the other. Each seemed to touch something inside me. Part of me wanted to laugh at the absurdity of it all. But I was too numb at that point to even smile. Most of me felt looming despair just out of reach, watching, waiting to smother me and infuse blackness into my heart. But I could actually cry no more than the tragedy mask could. I mimicked its anguished expression. Nothing came.

Instead, all the energy seemed to leach from my body. I wanted to crawl under the bed and hide—though, upon further inspection, I saw that the bed was too low. I had to settle for crawling under the covers.

The masks seemed to gaze down at me. I closed my eyes and sighed, not laughing or crying.

Then I fell asleep and did not dream.

A knock intruded.

11

OUT IN THE HALL, Ms. d'Aleu, fresh and rested, stood with two burdens: a box in her hands and unpleasant news written all over her face.

"Sleeping late, Miss Baker?" she said.

"It's Doctor Baker," I said. At least *she*, away from the guests, could address me properly.

"May I come in," she said, rather than asked. I hesitated, and she stepped right by me. "Close the door."

I closed it and faced her. "What time is it?"

"Six fifteen," she said.

I felt rested, but I also felt exhausted. And hungry. "I missed dinner?"

"You missed breakfast. Don't worry," she said. "I told them you had some business with me. We have a little time."

I wrapped my robe tighter around me to fend off a sudden chill. I tried to read her expression. Her eyes expressed concern, but her voice did not.

"Is there a problem?" I asked, hoping both that there was and I would be ejected from this situation, and at the same time that there wasn't, because I needed the money.

"There were concerns about your figure," she said.

"My figure!"

"Something about how you fit into your uniform."

I snorted. "That's rich. You gave me that uniform. It's not like I had any choice on the size."

"I know. That's why I brought this." She held up a box and gave me what I considered a devious grin.

I gave her and the box my best dubious look.

She sat on my bed and patted the space next to her. Sitting sounded like a great idea. I sat.

She opened the box. Inside was a black corset.

"Oh, no way!" I said.

"It will do wonders for you," she said cheerfully.

What was she? One of those *I am not a feminist* women? I said, "I fit in the uniform just fine!"

She didn't argue, just raised an eyebrow.

Suddenly I wasn't so sure. "Don't I?"

"You're going to love this," she said in an encouraging tone. "Feel the fabric."

Reluctantly I reached out and touched my hand to the sable brocade. I have to admit, it seemed like high quality.

She lifted it out of the box. "Feel the inside. Soft fabric. Women wear these all day. They're designed to be comfortable."

"They're designed to subjugate women," I said.

"Don't confuse subjugation of women with the sensuality of intimate fashion," she said in a soothing voice.

I said, "Don't confuse tailoring the dress to the woman with tailoring the woman to the dress."

"There's nothing wrong with a little shaping."

"'A little shaping,'" I said dryly. "Really."

"Women are subjugated all over the world," she said, "but it's not because of corsets. What we choose to wear is a private matter."

I nodded. "Yeah, so I choose not to wear this."

She put a hand to my cheek. "Don't take it like that, Melody. I'll bet soon you'll learn to love wearing it."

"That's easy for you to say! You're not the one to be pinched in half like a hot-dog link."

Ms. d'Aleu placed the box onto my lap—it was heavier than I expected—and stood before me.

Gazing into my eyes, she unbuttoned her gray flannel suit jacket, slipped off the red ribbon tied around her neck, and unbuttoned her plain silk white blouse. Underneath she was wearing a corset: plain beige cloth, no frills, with several vertical seams spaced every two inches all around. Beige struck me as an odd color for kink. Or was beige the new black?

I must be hallucinating, I thought because the corset seemed to have her slender torso shrunken down to the size of my calf. Nobody could be that thin!

"There's something wonderful about feeling the embrace of

your corset," she said in almost a whisper. "It makes you feel secure. Confident. Attractive. And it does wonders for your posture!"

I couldn't take my eyes off of her tiny waist.

"Go ahead," she said. "Touch it."

I reached out and with trembling fingers touched her abdomen. The fabric was firm and smooth—and warm, unlike her hands, which grasped mine in encouragement.

"Let's just try yours on," she said. "So you can see what it feels like."

She drew me up to my feet and slipped the robe off my shoulders. It dropped to the floor, leaving me completely naked before her. "Go on," she said with a smile. "I'll help."

I lifted out of the box the torture device and wrapped it around my waist. The thing was heavy! "What's it made of? Lead?"

"That's the steel boning," she told me.

I fastened a half dozen of metal loop closures in the front—the *busk*, she told me—and let the thing settle on my hips. "Hmmm, okay, I admit it. It's not so bad."

That was when Ms. d'Aleu tugged on the cords—the corset snugged around my waist.

Ooof!

"Everything all right?" she asked.

"Fine." Yeah, fine that I was being gussied up like some Victorian pinup!

She then drew the cords tighter—the corset cinched in. Okay, this is what corsets do, right? I tried to take a deep breath but ran up against the vise around my chest.

"Okay?" she asked.

"Okay," I half whispered, out of breath. The corset was now pretty tight and would take some serious getting used to.

Naturally, I thought we were finished, but she was saving the best for last and truly wrenched on the cords. Scarlett O'Hara had nothing on me then. I felt some tugging, and then an icy hand on my shoulder.

"You're about two inches from closed. That's a good start."

"'A good start'?"

She ran her hands up and down the corset. "Feel how it embraces you. The boning holds the shape and keeps it from riding up and pinching."

"Yeah, pinching would be bad," I wheezed.

"Notice how straight your posture is now."

"Because I have steel rods up my back."

She turned me around and looked at the corset on me. "You look delicious."

I looked down to see—but then she pushed me back, down onto the bed, and climbed up on top of me, straddling my cinched waist. She leaned over me, close. I thought she was going to say something, but she took a few silent moments looking me over with eyes dark with delight. "You have no idea how long I've wanted to have you in this position," she said.

Then she kissed me—a gentle touching of warm lips. My spine began tingling. I could feel myself blushing up and down. Instinctively I put my hands against her shoulders to push her away, but she seized my wrists and pinned them over my head. Now she was even closer.

"Ms. d'Aleu—"

She kissed me again.

And this time, I kissed back.

Yes, I kissed back, all right? I couldn't help it! I was at a disadvantage!

When she pulled away, she gazed at me with smoky eyes. "You are now mine, my dearest."

My heart jumped. I didn't know quite what she meant. "Uh, Ms. d'Aleu—"

"Whenever we are alone, you will address me as Mistress d'Aleu," she said in a stern voice. I blinked. "Or just Mistress, if you prefer."

"Mistress?"

"I give you this choice, Melody."

I'd felt overly formal saying Ms. d'Aleu already. "That's very generous of—"

She cut off my response with the hottest kiss I've ever had from any girl—from anyone. It was soft and hard and cold and hot. I could smell her sweet skin. I wanted to melt around her.

Suddenly she was off me, leaving me writhing, unsatiated.

Standing over me, she buttoned her blouse one button at a time, never taking her eyes off me.

I sat up, wanting another kiss.

She remained buttoned her jacket and gave me a wink.

Then she left. The door clicked shut behind her.

I flopped back and just lay there for a few minutes. My body was flushed. I think I was wet. Petra said I had to choose, and here was my body choosing for me.

But that Mistress crap is out!

12

*M*Y PULSE WAS RACING. I needed a cigarette. No, I didn't smoke, but I had the craving anyway. I had to settle for coffee.

A clean, fresh uniform (identical to the first) hung in the closet. I dressed, then made my way down the backstage stairs to the kitchen, where I met a gaunt woman, maybe thirty, with straight, dark brown hair, amber eyes, and dark ochre skin that gleamed under the LED lights. Her name was Anita. She was the sous-chef. She refused to give a last name.

"What do you need my last name for?" she said with a smile. "I am the only Anita in this alcázar."

In answer to my coffee quest, she directed me to a large brass samovar on the corner table in the kitchen. "I keep it stoked twenty-four hours a day," she said. "Life happens at all hours, and that means service happens at all hours, and that means people need coffee at all hours."

My first sip actually put a smile on my face. It was a deliciously rich dark roast with the slightest hint of what might have been cinnamon.

Things were looking up. Nothing like a good cup of joe to bring out the sunshine.

I was last to breakfast at the long unfinished table in the staff dining room just past the cellar door, but nobody mentioned it. All of the maids, along with Anita, Mrs. Skovde (or "Chef"), and her young, squat, spike-haired, sullen assistant, Ms. Cartwright, passed around serving plates laden with breakfast fare.

Ms. Metz, in a most casual, conversational tone, said, "You're glowing. Slept well?"

I wasn't thinking about sleep. I took a moment to reflect. "Yes."

"Have you lost weight?"

I thought of saying *Less volume*, but instead I just smiled, figuring I might as well enjoy an upside to being forced to wear this steampunk torture device.

I was starving. I loaded up my plate with scrambled eggs, three sausages, a big heap of potatoes, and a biscuit. But after a few mouthfuls, I couldn't eat any more. My stomach was squeezed down to the size of a pea, and that pea was stuffed to capacity.

"Not hungry after all?" asked Chef.

I smiled apologetically. "I guess my stomach shrank." I

wrapped my hands around my coffee. Cold drafts seemed to emanate from the walls, carrying a chill to my legs.

Ms. Metz said to everyone, "So we don't have to concern ourselves with the security team, but the Colonel's campaign staff arrives within the hour for their kickoff meeting, and they are to be treated as guests."

"Oh, dear Lord," said Ms. Odette with a note of spent hope.

Mrs. Phillips drew in a deep breath of apprehension. "Full service?"

"Buffet only," said Ms. Metz with a nod.

Mrs. Phillips exhaled in not quite a sigh. "Well, there's that, at least."

"Just as much work for us," Mrs. Skovde said, meaning the kitchen crew. Anita nodded. Ms. Cartwright just stared at her empty plate.

"This will be not what we're used to," Ms. Odette said, stress in her voice, her Jamaican accent becoming more pronounced. "The political campaign staff, they will be normal people." The way she said *normal* made them sound anything but. "These kinds of people, they do not live with service. They do not know what it is to be served."

"We don't have 'kinds of people,'" said Ms. Metz in a hush. "We have guests."

Ms. Odette continued. "At first, these kinds of people—"

Ms. Metz sucked her teeth.

"—they will be grateful for your service. They will say, 'Thank you,' and, 'You are so kind.' Some will even try to help by bringing their dishes into this kitchen."

Mrs. Phillips let loose a nasal note of skepticism.

"But soon, maybe after a few days, they will help a little less
. . . until they do nothing and leave it all to you."

Ms. Vitiello grunted. "And then they're like everyone else
we serve."

"No," Ms. Odette said, almost as if scolding. "Remember,
these kinds of people are normal people. They have not been
raised with manners, with appreciation, with dignity."

I had to speak up there. "So I'm normal, and that means I
have no dignity?"

Ms. Odette, without easing her intensity, smiled warmly.
"No, no, no, you, I, we—like them—if we come from good
homes, and have good teachers, we learn courtesy. We learn
the Golden Rule."

"Those with the gold make the rules," I said.

"Even if they're idiots," Mrs. Phillips said.

Ms. Odette ignored us and said, "Do unto others as you
would have them do unto you. But"—she shook her head in
apparent disappointment—"these kinds of people, after becoming accustomed to being served, they will take you for granted.
Not all of them, but many of them will leave dishes on the floor.
Others will leave garbage everywhere. Some will be rude."

"Rude?" I said dryly. "No, really?"

Ms. Odette fixed her eyes on me. "It is a different kind of
rudeness, yes?"

"Rude is rude," I said.

That got a laugh from her, but after a moment, I realized I
was the joke.

She said, "The Colonel's friends, his regular guests, people
of his class, they are rude and indifferent because they think

they are better. And why should they not think that? We do not threaten them."

The knot in my stomach twisted. I would have taken a deep breath, but the vise strapped around my waist would not give an inch.

"The normal people," she continued, "when they are introduced to being served all the time, they *want* to think they are better than us. But deep in their hearts, they know they are not." She put her hand on her own chest. "They feel this. It hurts, they hurt, and they do not know it. They do not think it in their minds. But it hurts. And with that comes resentment. Toward us."

We all looked at one another. *Great. I'm stuck here in this stone fortress with a paramilitary battalion ready to get into bigger and better fights while we get to serve a bunch of resentful peasants like me, who will want to think they're better than I am, and hate me because they are not.*

Mrs. Phillips asked, "It sounds like you've been through this before, Ms. Odette."

"I have," she said. "Before the Colonel, I worked for a Wall Street trader who made billions in credit default swaps. He and his friends, they could not enjoy service because they always had to prove to themselves that they deserved it."

"People are people," Ms. Metz said, getting up and clearing her place. "Here in the Colonel's home we have guests, and they have service. We all have jobs to do, and ours is to get this brunch buffet in place for the Colonel and his campaign staff. Let's get to work."

Ms. Odette gave a wise nod. "Watch and see."

13

W<small>E WERE PREPARED FOR</small> the worst, so it was all a bit of a shock for the normally unflappable service staff (and very flappable me) to be greeted by the first arrivals as peers, not peons. If not for Ms. Odette's occasional raised eyebrow (shared for our eyes only), we might have been lulled into a sense of *égalité et fraternité*.

"Call me R.D.," Roy Dean Lonnigan drawled as he shook hands with each and every one of us in the foyer. "Are you registered to vote? It takes no time at all. Talk to me if you need a hand."

Once that was done with felicitations, he openly marveled at the decor. "Lovely place. Wonderful!" That he was the campaign's field director must have explained his well-honed, friendliest-of-friendly friending skills.

As I showed him into the library, he said, "I can see I'm going to enjoy working here." His eyes fell to my legs. "And what's your name?"

"I am Miss Baker."

"What's your first name?" he asked, not missing a beat, and his friendliest-of-friendly demeanor led me to blunder into dropping my guard.

"Melody, but we use formal address here, so you can just call me Miss Baker."

"It is a *pleasure* to meet you, Melody. May I call you Mel?"

"You may call me Miss Baker."

He took my hand into both of his and didn't let go. How so very not charming.

I said, "I must get back to work."

"Of course, Mel. I look forward to seeing you again."

I extricated my hand from his grasp. "The Colonel is holding the meeting here in the library. We've set up a beverage bar with French-roast coffee and a variety of teas. Please help yourself."

He turned to look. I made my escape.

In the foyer, the staff was dealing with another friendly sort: Hazel Foyle, a peach-cheeked, banana-haired woman who not only offered her own gregarious salutations but, once she was relieved of her Brooks Brothers overcoat, gave every one of us a hug. "I'm a hugger," she helpfully explained as she waved each of us, one by one, into her arms. "Come on. Everyone gets a hug!" Her embrace was gentle and just longer than cursory. She smelled of corn chips. I tried to imagine Hazel Foyle hugging the Colonel, but couldn't.

She had an assistant with her: a skinny, pale boy burdened with an unfortunate case of acne and five fully loaded five-inch ring binders that threatened to find their own places on the marble floor. Fortunately, once Mrs. Foyle was finished with all of us, she rescued him, wrapping her arms around the binders and lifting them off of his crumpling form.

"Come, Max," she said, marching into the library. "Let's find a home for these." He followed behind, using his freed hands to pick at his zits.

For all of Hazel Foyle's gregarious embraces, she proved the amiable exception to the disagreeable rule—typified by Virgil Kredic, the campaign treasurer, who entered the castle with a haughty air, as if trying to impress someone with his royal dignity, and thus convincing everyone (on staff, at least) of his lack of either.

Mr. Kredic strolled into the center of the foyer with head held high—as high as his five-foot-two-inch frame would allow—and swept his imperious gaze around at all of us. Then he threw out his arms, presumably to have his coat removed, but giving the definite impression that he was waiting to be fitted for crucifixion. Ms. Vitiello stifled a giggle.

Mrs. Phillips had to force his arms down to relieve him of his polyester-blend overcoat. "What the devil!" he cried as she tried to wrestle the garment off.

"It would help if you'd lower your arms, sir," she said.

It took nearly a minute, and once she succeeded, he put out his hand. "Claim check?"

Mrs. Phillips's eyebrows went up at least an inch. She gave a humph and took his finery into the cloakroom.

"Don't expect a tip," he said in what no doubt was intended to be a devastating tone.

Daisy Waukenish was in every way the opposite of Mr. Kredic, and not only because he was as white as dried milk while she, the only African-American on the campaign staff, had blue-black skin darker than beluga caviar. He, as campaign treasurer, spent money that she, as finance director, raised. He was short, skinny, and balding, while she was tall, round, and blessed with a mane of beautiful curly black hair as big as an unfurled umbrella. He drank black coffee and ate nothing, while she consumed bottled springwater and ate two bags of fried beet chips she brought with her.

Another early arrival was Tatiana Willoughby. I don't think Ms. Willoughby, or Tati, as she preferred to be called, spoke at all for the first three or four hours, and only rarely after that. Throughout the meeting, as well as during breaks, Tati was constantly looking at and tapping her phone, which I suppose was appropriate for the new-media director.

At ten on the dot, most everyone had arrived, and the Colonel called the meeting to order, welcomed everybody, and promptly turned the floor over to Angela Thorndike.

Ms. Thorndike was the campaign director, and she made sure everyone knew it—not by declaring, "I am the campaign director," but by promenading around like she was the Duchess of Duchess County and the Party was *her* Party. I'd seen her type before, in my father's campaigns: efficient, effective, pragmatic, ruthless, and apolitically opportunistic—all process and no heart. Unlike the other night, when she'd presumably been campaigning for the job, during this meeting she feigned an uppah-clahss New Englahnd ahccent and held her nose high in matching affect.

The people near her likewise raised their noses—but to avoid her pungent apricot cologne. I casually positioned myself to gain some distance from those heavy molecules that were charging off of her rabbit-wrapped neck and marauding my poor olfactory nerves.

The meeting droned on and on, mostly with Ms. Thorndike guiding everyone through ground rules and points of concern, while others sounded off only occasionally—a fugue of egos dominated by Ms. Thorndike's oboe-like voice.

Mr. Kredic spread sour disapprobation in the few times he did speak. Throughout the campaign meeting, he was just as stiff about finances. "Only I shall sign all checks. Only I shall approve all wires. I run a tight ship. *Nothing* without a *line* in the *budget* gets spent, or heads will *roll*."

A few eyes rolled at that. Not the Colonel's, though. He suppressed a smile and glanced at Mr. Henderson next to him, apparently entertained by Mr. Kredic's display of insecure command. *Is this what the Colonel wanted?*

Ms. Waukenish's loquacious comments filled the room with optimism. Anything was possible, in her view.

Even so, most of the others didn't seem to lend her much credence.

And nobody was willing to try her chips.

"What are they? Red potato?" R.D. asked.

"Beet chips," she said with a grin. "They boost your energy."

R.D.'s face soured. "I truly appreciate the offer, but I must forbear."

She turned to her other side. "How about you, Mr. Kredic?"

"No," he snipped.

Undeterred, she held out the open bag to him. "Are you sure? They're a great source of iron."

"My iron is sufficient, thank you," Mr. Kredic said with not a drop of thank you anywhere in his tone.

At that point, she just smiled—a class act in the presence of classless slights.

"I'll try some chips," the Colonel said, already rising from his chair. He crossed over to Ms. Waukenish.

She held out the bag. "Some people like them with dip, but I prefer them just like this."

The Colonel fished out two or three chips, said, "Thank you."

"I hope you like them."

He popped the beet chips into his mouth. Everyone watched for a reaction. He chewed. He swallowed. "May I impose . . . ?"

She smiled and nodded. He took a few more chips and walked back to his seat. I heard him mutter to Mr. Henderson, "Here, try one of these."

Mr. Henderson said, "Are they good?"

I heard crunching. A quick glance told me Mr. Henderson was chomping on the snack. He gave me a friendly wink.

Tati's two contributions were complete non sequiturs. During discussion of finances and Party-sourced campaign funds, she blurted, "Yes! One hundred thousand followers," triggering disapproving looks from Virgil Kredic and Daisy Waukenish— the one time those two agreed on anything.

Tati's other contribution was right in the middle of Hazel Foyle's get-out-the-vote plans, when Tati sighed and said to her phone, "Oh! Go ahead, unfollow!"

She didn't seem to have been experiencing any trouble getting a data signal.

Her non sequiturs were nothing compared to those of Spizz. That was his name. Just Spizz. No first name, last name. No Mister. His hair sprouted out of his scalp and chin in haphazard directions. His shirt's wrinkles attested to his indifference to ironing. At first I thought he had just gotten out of bed, but as the day went on, he never seemed to fully wake up or tidy up. It sometimes took him several minutes before answering a question or responding to a statement—which was odd, given that he was the campaign's event scheduler. But I guess it worked. Nothing seemed to get by him. He would get around to reacting . . . eventually. Maybe he had slow neurons.

"When is the Colonel's first appearance in Albany?" R.D. asked at one point.

Spizz cocked his head and said nothing. R.D. asked again but got no response. Eventually he gave up, and the conversation moved on to the Colonel's formal announcement in New York City. "That's happening at a hotel, I forget where," said R.D.

"Next week on Wednesday," Spizz said.

"No, it's tomorrow," Ms. Doyle said.

"Albany," Spizz said.

"No, I *know* it's in Manhattan," R.D. said.

"The Plaza," Spizz said.

After a while, everyone learned to backtrack through recent conversations to see where Spizz's latest utterances might fit.

Much more plain spoken was Cale Plumout. This freckled, eighteen-year-old geek with an Alfalfa haircut, vacant eyes, and a bad case of halitosis claimed the title of technology ninja. His online handle—"bowtiesarefreedom"— was no doubt a grand declaration of his worldview, or at least his neckwear.

His moniker also seemed to reflect his maturity. During a discussion about the campaign website, bowtiesarefreedom shouted down Mr. Henderson about the color palette.

"Black websites are hot! What do you know about web development?"

Mr. Henderson walked right up to him. I thought he was going to deck the kid right there. "Is that a clip-on tie?" he asked.

Master Plumout jutted out his chin. "So? It's the *effect* that matters."

Mr. Henderson yanked the bow tie off of the tech ninja's collar. "The *effect* seems to be lack of commitment." He tossed it onto Master Plumout's lap.

Several laughed.

Master Plumout turned pink and cried in defiance, "How many hours of your life have you wasted tying ties?"

Mr. Henderson resumed his seat. "Sometimes the shortcuts aren't worth it, kid."

Around mid-afternoon, when conversation turned to production of the campaign's TV ads, a stone-faced man with wild, gray eyebrows, dyed black hair, and pasty white skin with liver spots that contrasted with his shiny black Italian-cut suit sounded off: "Fuck 'em."

This was Mr. Mort Rogers, the world-famous litigation attor-

ney, expressing his no-doubt expensive legal opinion when Reg
Mills, the communications director, noted that the campaign
just signed a contract with Flem Media—creators of the cen-
tipede-with-a-smartphone ad for Gene Smitlick in Michigan
and the famous flying pig ad that nearly got Bazoo Bootkins
elected governor of Arkansas—but the Party had committed
to Rim & Gross Advertising for all campaign television spots,
and Rim & Gross was now threatening to sue.

"Fuck 'em and fuck their lawyers," Mr. Rogers said.

I thought about Ms. d'Aleu. What kind of lawyer was she?
I pictured her facing off against Mr. Rogers in a grand show-
down. Beauty versus the beast.

R.D. said, "But the Party money is tied to the contract."

Mr. Rogers started gesturing with one hand. "Let them try to
enforce it. We take the money and fuck Rim & Gross. What are
they going to do? Sue us? They can bend over and take three
years of discovery. How deep are their pockets? They're tiny.
They're ants. They're less than ants. They're . . . what do you
call those things that live in your bed?"

Someone said, "Escorts?"

Someone else said, "Bedbugs."

Ms. Waukenish said, "Mites."

"That's it," Mr. Rogers said. "Mites. They're as mighty as
mites that are smaller than ants. Fuck 'em."

I tried to picture Mr. Rogers fucking a mite.

14

THE ORANGE SUNSET WAS just shifting toward the blue of twilight when, in the middle of a discussion of the best way to pitch a plan for K–12 children to bring pistols to school "for protection in the bathroom," the Colonel abruptly stood and said, "The Hang Seng and Shanghai are about to open. Mr. Henderson and I have some fun business to take care of. I leave everything in your capable hands."

And with that, he ambled out of the library.

Mr. Henderson said, "Don't stay up too late, kids," and followed.

Once they were gone, the tenor of the meeting changed.

"Jesus, I thought he'd never leave," said Mr. Rogers.

Tati tapped rapidly on her phone. "I wonder what they're up to . . ."

R.D. sighed and sank back into his chair. "How long do you think this campaign is going to last?"

"My people don't give him long," said Ms. Waukenish. "They're very hesitant to write any checks. I don't know what to tell the Colonel."

"Tell him to write his own checks."

She said, "Nothing opens up the checkbooks like winning. Does anyone here plan on winning?"

"Winning?" said R.D. "He has to beat Lane Tibbs in the primary first."

"Tibbs will be nothing. He has no money. Focus on November. Focus on Melvin Milford."

"I'm counting on Tibbs," said R.D. in a tone far from affable.

Spizz said, "Good night, Colonel."

Ms. Thorndike coughed deliberately.

R.D. glanced at her and said, "I mean, don't get me wrong. I appreciate this job. But I already have a position lined up with the Thud presidential campaign for the general."

Ms. Waukenish let out a *humph*. "You're going to work for The Johnson?"

"Hey, Johnson Thud tells it like it is."

"In his own dreams."

"Oh, fuck Johnson Thud," said Mr. Rogers.

"You're going to have to start watching what you say, Mort," said R.D. "Mark my words. Johnson Thud is the future."

Mort gave a hmmph. "Johnson Thud is a charlatan. He's not a real conservative."

Mr. Kredic suddenly stood. "Conservative conschmervative! What do I care from conservatives?" He shuffled over to the coffee stand. "R.D. is right. A new day is coming, people. New leadership. Effective leadership from a businessman. He'll clean up this government. Secure the borders. And then we can get down to the real business. We're finally going to have some law and order and clean out America's streets of the filth and scum."

Silence fell—from embarrassment or quiet assent, I couldn't tell. Probably a bit of both.

As an afterthought, Mr. Kredic half-turned his head toward Ms. Waukenish and said, "Nothing personal, Daisy."

Ms. Waukenish put on a smile. "Of course, Virgil. None taken." Me, I wasn't convinced.

But Mr. Kredic seemed to take her words at face value. With a contented smile that worked against all the frown lines and scowl cracks in his face, he took his coffee back to his seat and said quietly to her, "You're one of the good ones."

At that, Ms. Waukenish looked at him with an implacable expression and said, "You almost make me want to say something similar."

Mr. Kredic thought about that a moment. He sipped his coffee.

Ms. Thorndike said, "All right, we aren't going to solve Party schisms here. Just keep your heads." Her gaze swept around to focus on each of the campaign staffers, one by one. "We will keep pushing right to appeal to the voters. We get a bump in the primary polls. We look good. And only once the Colonel loses will any of you make any moves. Understood?"

There were nods all around.

"So let's run down our positions on the issues. I want to be able to tell him what he stands for by morning."

Wouldn't want to bother the candidate with trivial things like what he believes, would we?

We on the service staff took turns taking short breaks, during which times we would wolf down a bit of sandwich or relieve ourselves of nature's call. I welcomed even brief respites from the inane blathering of these politicos.

Otherwise we spent our minutes chasing down diet soda re-fills and cans of energy drinks while fielding endless "small requests": No, we did not have any Caffeine Tar Energy Chew. No, we did not have any bacon-wrapped donuts. No, we did not have spray-on cheese food for the sandwiches. "Does Somerset Cheddar not suffice?" Apparently not.

I'd been sixteen hours on my feet by the time the campaign staff began to wrap up their meeting. As far as I was concerned, they couldn't get out fast enough. I didn't want to take another step. My feet in the pumps appeared to be fine, but in my mind's eye, they were bloody stumps jammed into garlic presses. And I needed a bath.

Finally the last of them departed the castle, off to crawl back under the rocks from which they'd emerged.

And I crawled upstairs. This spy was to debrief with the Colonel.

15

*I*N THE FOUR DAYS since being hired, I'd been mocked, berated, flirted with, ignored, molested by Teddy Snoot, seduced and cinched by Ms. d'Aleu, evicted from my apartment, robbed by my landlord, mugged by security, and to top it all off, subjected to some of the most inane political planning by Washington wonks, many of whom were unscrupulous, opportunistic, bigoted weasels, so I didn't stand on ceremony once I stepped inside the Colonel's office. I yanked off my pumps—revealing no bloody stumps, but there were a couple of promising blisters—crossed over to the same chair as before, and sank into its cushions. I wasn't sure how much more of this job I could take.

The Colonel proffered a cognac. I quaffed it—

—and exhaled. It was peaceful in there, the only sound the slow, quiet *tick . . . tock . . .* of the grandfather clock's pendulum.

"So," said the Colonel.

I opened my eyes.

He gave me an intrigued look, and a smile spread across his face. "Have I told you why I'm running for senate?"

Uh oh. "No," I said and prepared myself for a big speech full of idealistic rhetoric about hope for the future, time to clean up Washington, "I am John Galt," blah, blah, blah.

He gulped his cognac and said in a clear voice, "Because I'm a fool."

I blurted a laugh and cut it off.

He smiled, took my empty glass, and went to the bar. "I'm no politician," he said while pouring. "I don't know the ins and outs of congressional rules, or legislative practices, or intraparty dynamics—that's what aides are for."

He handed me a fresh snifter. My grateful nose took in the fragrance.

"But I do know that we don't live in a Frank Capra film," he said. "It takes more to change the world than idealism and innocence."

Feeling warm and secure inside, I asked, "So what will you be bringing to the Party?"

"Manners."

He had to be kidding. "Manners?"

"Manners," he said, not at all kidding. He started to pace. "Politics has become an ugly spectacle that debases us all— everyone, the liars and innocents, the power brokers and the poverty-stricken voters. What we need is a restoration of manners."

"As in etiquette?"

"Oh, of course there's etiquette, but it's more than that. Having manners is a way of life, a philosophy, a way of doing business, a way of friendship, a way of dealing with one's enemies."

I thought I'd offer a bit of literary wit. "Ambrose Bierce defined politeness as 'the most acceptable hypocrisy.'"

"Hypocrisy?" He turned to me and frowned. "That's rather harsh. The uncharitable description of manners would be more 'the art of lying in benign ways, so as not to offend or make someone uncomfortable.' Manners keep things civil. Heads cool. So that society can progress."

I figured he must have had a head start on the cognac. "So that's all it takes? Some manners?"

He nodded. "The things money can't buy. Manners. Morals. Trust. Integrity."

I sipped my drink before asking, "Does your campaign staff know this?"

"Oh, hell no. They want me to run because it will bring some excitement into their lives. And the big-shot decision makers you met the other night want me because I don't need to raise funds to present as a viable candidate on such short notice. And they all like that I'm nothing like Frank Detton, may he rest in peace." Detton, the front-runner who had just died. "These political geniuses," the Colonel said with a note of sarcasm, "see an opportunity to rebrand the party, at least here in New York, and they think the way to achieve that is through someone like me."

He seemed to be in a loquacious mood, so I asked, "Why Angela Thorndike?"

He took the question in stride. "She's a very accomplished campaign manager, with fourteen wins," he recited—apparently parroting what he had heard. He didn't seem all that certain about it, but his shrug—very un-Petra-like—indicated he was resigned to his fate with Ms. Thorndike. "I've been told we are extremely fortunate to have her leading our team."

I could let that statement lie there, and I was tired, cranky, my feet hurt, and I was drinking cognac, so I said, "I thought the staff gets behind the candidate, not the other way around."

He put out his hand for my glass. I gave it to him, and he took it to the bar for a third round. He said, "We don't have the luxury of time in putting this campaign together. Thorndike comes most highly recommended."

"I work for you, Colonel, so I hesitate to say—" *that she's batshit crazy.* "After you left tonight, she was pushing some odd ideas."

He handed me a tall cognac. "Remember, Baker, given your background, your father's politics, you are not familiar with our Party. New ideas are going to sound strange."

"New ideas? Like religious rights for corporations?"

He raised a hand at that. "Corporate personhood is a long-standing legal principle," he said, very professorially. "It's one of the most empowering progressive contributions America has made to the modern era."

I couldn't help myself. "And corporations have First Amendment rights?"

He looked at me warily. "Yes."

I asked, "Do corporations kneel for communion?"

He waved his hand in dismissal.

I pressed. "Do Jewish corporations have bar mitzvahs? But wait, are corporations male or female? Maybe it would be bat mitzvahs."

"Now you're just being ridiculous."

"Am I? Can a Muslim corporation impose sharia law on its workers?"

"The religious-rights thing is an unfortunate red herring. My focus is on the beneficial aspects corporate personhood affords for business opportunity."

"Do corporations get to collect Social Security?"

"Well, I think the plan is that we'd do away with Social Security and institute private retirement accounts."

"Do corporations retire?"

He laughed politely. "This is very entertaining, Baker," he said—meaning he was not entertained.

But I was feeling my liquor, and I was on a roll. "Do corporations have to serve jury duty? Do corporations have to register for the draft? They'd have to be eighteen years old first, I suppose. Can corporations marry? We already have mergers. I suppose those would be considered civil unions. Can a corporation marry a human person? Or are they restricted to marrying only other corporations? Would that stand in light of *Obergefell v. Hodges* and *Loving v. Virginia*? I suppose corporate acquisitions would be out altogether." I paused for rhetorical effect. "A hostile takeover would be tantamount to slavery."

The Colonel huffed. "I never figured you to be an Occupy type, Baker. Corporations are an essential part of free enterprise. They enable entrepreneurs to take risks, to take a chance on a dream without risking the ruin of their families."

"And the regular citizens," I said, "they get what? Debtors' prisons?"

"Nobody is talking about debtors' prisons."

He was getting irritated, but I was just getting going. My commentary's incisiveness was dialed to eleven. "We'd have to lock up sixty million people," I said. "On the other hand, imagine all the license plates we could produce!"

The Colonel rubbed his brow. "I wish you would take this seriously. I am running not because I agree with the entire Party platform, but I do believe in a general philosophy that our best way forward is to return to our core principles enshrined in the Constitution."

"Okay," I said and decided to drop the argumentum ad absurdum. It was time to get to the point.

I was either a spy or I wasn't. I had to lay it out there.

I swallowed the rest of my cognac and tossed out the bomb: "Do you know that most of your campaign staff is expecting you to lose the primary?"

"I'm sure you're exaggerating."

"They figure you have no chance against Lane Tibbs."

"That idiot?"

"Several plan to join Johnson Thud's campaign."

"Don't be ridiculous, Baker. They're putting together a great campaign for me. I'll write some checks. They'll crank out some commercials. Tibbs won't stand a chance."

I didn't want to demoralize him, so I offered a Jeeves-like, "If you say so, Colonel."

Now the Colonel seemed to get a bit worked up. "I can't believe anyone would want to campaign for Johnson Thud. He's an even bigger idiot than Tibbs. No political ideas whatsoever."

I said, "I think you're wrong, Colonel."

He turned on me. "Oh, so you think the bilge he's peddling is profound? A PhD from Columbia should know better."

"I'm looking at the subtext," I said.

The Colonel finished his cognac and put out his hand for my empty glass. "Aren't you overestimating the voters, Baker?" He stepped to the bar. "They aren't reading subtext."

"They're picking up on something."

"They won't be able to help but pick up on our message. I'll be spending millions selling it."

"You're selling, Colonel, but what if the voters aren't buying?"

"They're buying something," the Colonel said. "Look at all the morons supporting Thud."

He handed me a fresh cognac. I sipped it, considering how to put this. I was probably going to get fired for all the shit I was saying. Obviously I wasn't coming from the same political realm as the Colonel.

But maybe that was exactly why he needed to hear what I had to say. At the worst, I'd earn the ten grand he advanced me.

"Johnson Thud isn't selling anything," I said.

"Not anything coherent, anyway," said the Colonel.

Now it was my turn to get professorial. "A famous writer once remarked that the guest on a talk show is not really a guest, he's really the stooge. The real guest is the audience who make comments about the person on stage. That's why people tune in. To get the audience's take on the stooge."

The Colonel waved his hand. "I'll take your word for it. I could never stand talk shows. The profundity of mediocre thinking."

"That is exactly what Thud is doing. He's acting as host, and the stooge is the government itself."

The Colonel raised a hand in defense. "Baker, I know you liberals like to think that conservatives are lunatics who want to just destroy government."

"That's been your rhetoric for decades."

"We say it. But nobody really believes it."

"The Thud voters do."

"Thud isn't even a real conservative."

"But that doesn't matter. He's not selling himself. He's hosting a show. Johnson Thud is just spouting off what these voters are saying already. They don't want Party apparatchiks." I smiled to myself—I used a Petra word. "They want to be heard, and The Johnson hears them. They go to the rallies because they're the guests who get heard. I bet they go to experience being together as much as to see him."

The Colonel looked at me sideways. "I assume you aren't saying that I should just do what Thud is doing."

"No," I said. "But your staff is right. You won't get anywhere with the campaign your staff is putting together. They're steering you right into a ditch."

"But they're the experts."

I gulped down the last of my cognac. My head was floating a few inches above my shoulders. I was just numb enough to accept being fired. "They're experts in losing," I said. "Forget everything your campaign staff and focus groups and Party officials say. Kids can smell bullshit. Run on what you believe in. Manners, integrity, all that. And if you lose, at least you did it on your own terms."

"You think that's true even in this age of of Johnson Thud?"

"Especially so," I said.

The Colonel peered into his cognac and said nothing for a full minute.

I waited. *He's searching for a polite way to fire me.* At least I'd had my say. I just couldn't let those campaign wonks play the Colonel for a paycheck without telling him. I did my duty as a spy, even if I was an awful maid.

The Colonel cleared his throat. *Here it comes.* I took a deep breath in preparation.

"So, Baker . . ." he began, and drifted off for a few seconds. This was really proving to be hard for him. I considered making it easy and telling him that I quit, but something held me back. I guess I was taking my own advice: facing the consequences on my own terms.

"This has been a great talk, Baker. You're right. I know nothing about how people really live. That's why I need you."

What? A spark of hope ignited in my chest. "As your assistant?"

"Oh, no, of course not. Nobody would have you, given your father's prominent place in the opposition. No, you stay as a maid. Be my eyes and ears. And we'll debrief every night."

I thought about it. My feet were still throbbing. But the cognac was good. And if the Colonel really was going to take my advice, maybe this maiding job would get interesting.

Besides, where else could I go?

"Okay, Colonel, you have a deal," I said.

Or to put it into Mr. Rogers' parlance: Fuck Ms. Thorndike. This campaign now belonged to me.

The story continues in
The Candidate's Maid, Book Three: *Of Tea and Conspiracy*
(Summer 2016)

ACKNOWLEDGMENTS

This book began years ago as a single paragraph that then sat in the metaphorical drawer until I didn't remember writing it anymore. A couple of years ago, as our politics entered a new phase, I dusted it off and wrote a complete novel. Unfortunately, or fortunately, after I set the manuscript aside to get some distance, the politics of this country continued to evolve, rapidly outstripping even the most outrageous and over-the-top satire I had in that draft. This book is a reboot.

Without my editor and best friend, Katherine M. Lawrence, this book would not exist at all. Her criticism, insightful editing, instincts, and unrelenting dedication have helped me persevere through this process.

Gratitude goes to Tiffany Yates Martin, FoxPrint Editorial, for her editorial work on an early draft.

Greatly valued with my appreciation are Tonia Hurst, whose feedback I value highly.

Special and heartfelt thanks go to readers Crystal Thieringer, Roslynn Pryor, Janet Brantley, and Carolyn Studer for their sharp and timely feedback as I was blasting out that first draft.

Finally, I would not be writing fictional tales were it not for the steady and unwavering encouragement, support, and love from my mother, whose critical mind and poetic soul are constant inspirations, my sister, whose strength and tenacity humbles me, my beautiful niece, who at fifteen years old is outpacing everything I've done, and my late father, who always wanted the best for me and never let me forget my creative endeavors. Love you all!

—LLS, *Boulder*

About the Author

Over the years, Laura Lis Scott has (yes) waited tables, delivered campus mail, driven a truck (more like a van), wordprocessed business and legal documents, written and produced videos, produced B-movie trailers, directed television, designed and developed websites, edited magazine articles, created logos, blogged amateurly (often amateurishly) and professionally, co-founded a few companies, raced cars (on actual racetracks—street racing is dumb), and written a handful of stories.

When she's not writing her own stuff, Laura serves as the editor for Katherine M. Lawrence's Yamabuki novels set in 12th-century Japan.

Laura has BA from The University of Chicago and an MFA from Columbia University of New York. Alas, she has no PhD; she hopes you'll forgive her for that. She lives in Colorado, where the sun always shines, even on the cloudy days.

The Candidate's Maid is her first novel. Before that, she just shouted at the television.

Laura's links:

¶ website: LauraLisScott.com

¶ Facebook: www.facebook.com/lauralisscott

¶ Twitter: @lauralisscott

¶ Subscribe to Laura's newsletter at eepurl.com/NyRDb

About Toot Sweet Ink

Toot Sweet Ink is an imprint of Toot Sweet Inc., independent publishers based in Boulder, Colorado.

Watch for our upcoming releases in science fiction, non-fiction, women's contemporary fiction, humor, and historical fiction, including the series of samurai novels by Katherine M. Lawrence, which follow the adventures of Yamabuki, a woman warrior in 12th-century Japan.

Twitter: @TootSweetInk

Facebook: www.facebook.com/tootsweetink

Website: TootSweet.ink

Newsletter: Get updates and learn about new releases and discount opportunities on our upcoming titles by signing up at eepurl.com/K8XVn